Will Y...

words by Robyn Opie
illustrated by Rory Stapleton

"Will you play with me?"
said the dog.

"I'm too busy," said the cat.

"Will you play with me?"
said the dog.

"I'm too busy," said the duck.

"Will you play with me?"
said the dog.

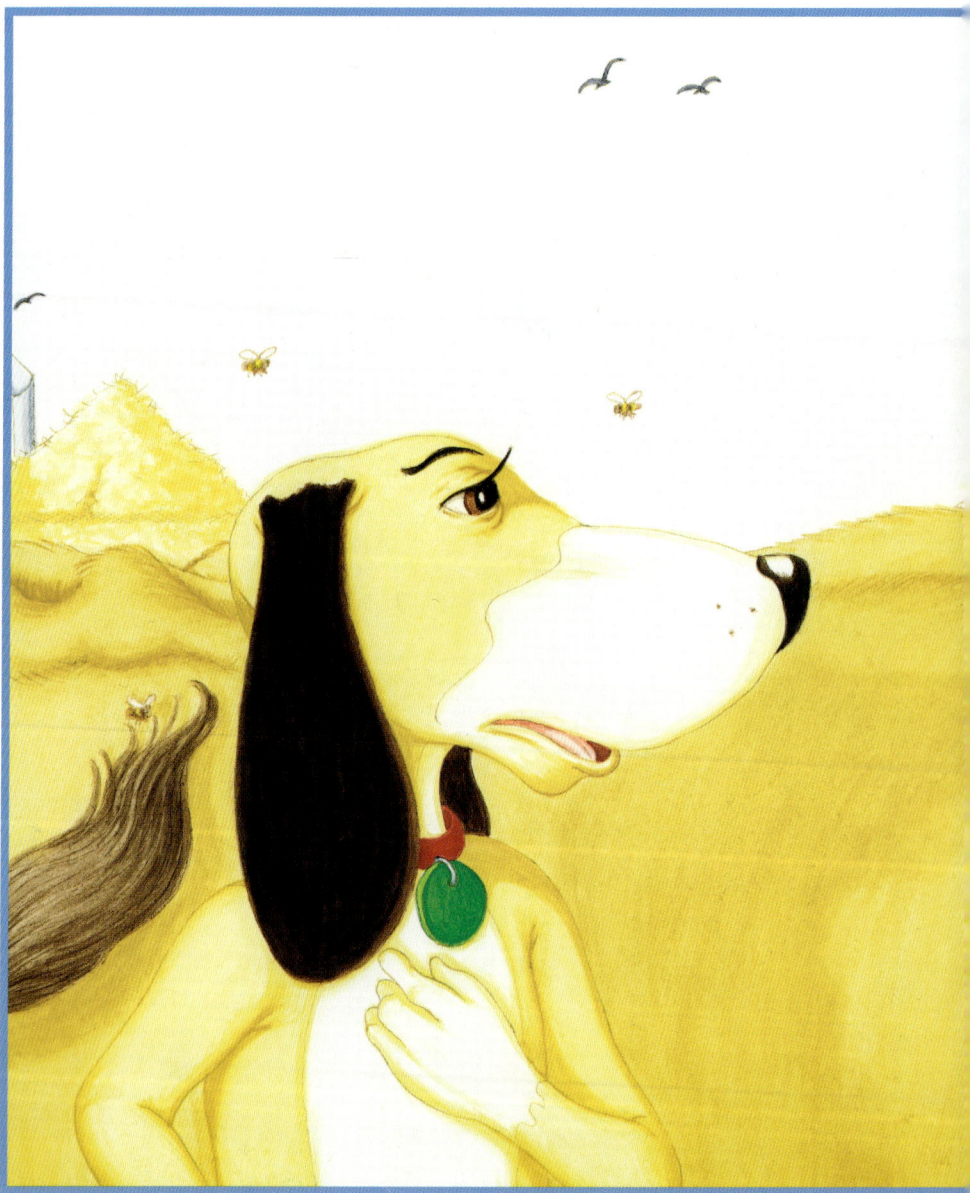

"I'm too busy," said the cow.

"Will you play with me?"
said the dog.

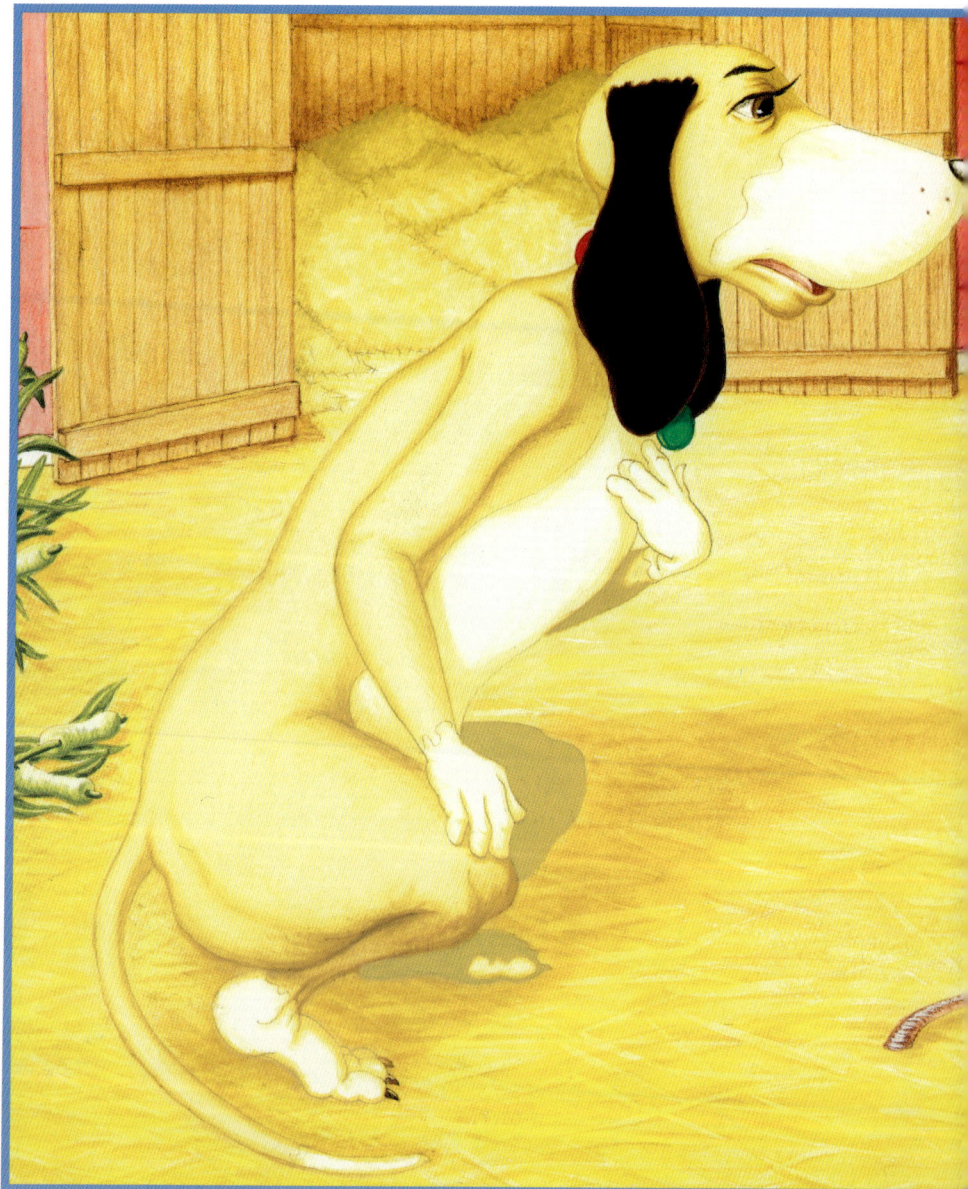

"Yes," said the hen.

The dog and the hen
went in to the barn.

They played in the barn.

The dog and the hen had fun.

The cat went to look.

The duck and the cow
went to look.

"Will you play with us?"
they all said.